I0713406

PUBLISHED by
PARABLES
Earthly Stories with a Heavenly Meaning

RANDALL LECHNER

THE
LORD'S PRAYER

Tiitle: The Lord's Prayer
Author: Randall Lechner
Copyright © Randall Lechner
September, 2017

Published By Parables
September, 2017

ISBN 978-1-945698-30-9
Printed in the United States of America

Readers should be aware that Internet Web sites offered as citations and/or sources for further information may have been changed or disappeared between the time this was written and when it is read.

RANDALL LECHNER

THE
LORD'S PRAYER

You must first learn to "Be" before you can "Do"

Grandpa Randy at his lake house in Petersburg Illinois, where this book was finished, but note… It was started on The KATY bike Trail in St Charles, Mo. To all my kids and grandchildren, both present and yet to come, I love you with all the love that a human heart can have, and miss you very much. I look forward to Eternity where we never say goodbye and can play together forever.

FORWARD

It was a dark and dreary day in Mr. Hadley's art class, my junior year in high school, as I recall. The subject for the quarter was silk screening: how to draw cut and make a screen to print a T-shirt. Yes, this was back in the era of B.C. (before computers),1970. Screen printing was a virtually unknown commercial profession, but still very much a hidden art form. A creative and challenging fun one, to say the least. It was then and there that I decided what I wanted to do for a career: print T-shirts. The ideas were coming unlimited as to other things you could screen, yet to be invented.

Against all odds and advice, I knew what I wanted to do with my artistic talent.

It was that very day that I sat down and made a list of the accomplishments I wanted to achieve before turning the ancient age of 40.

Now, at age 57, I can say I have accomplished 90% of what I set out **NOT** to do. The Silk Screen career was one that was accomplished, but not without a price.

Yes, Life Happened, and for the most part, I am still learning that, regardless of man's best intentions and plans, unless they are given to and controlled by the Holy Spirit, they become mostly just that…man's plans.

I regret that it has taken me so many years to realize what is necessary to mature, heal and make life work.

As the book of Proverbs states, *"The plans of a man are in his heart, but the Lord directs his path."* Proverbs 16:1

I thank God for the talents, abilities, creativity, and intelligence He has given me, that I may eventually learn HIS ways vs. mine. Isaiah 55:8-9.

I am most thankful for My Family, Kids, and Grandkids, whom forever give new life to an old world that just keeps cycling, whether we like it or not.

I pray that the knowledge I have learned the last half century will be much quicker and golden than the years that I am presently attaining. May you who read this be blessed beyond measure, for it is truly a labor of love for those I miss the most: Kaden, Ryan, Kai, Grayson, Maddox, Garrett, and my princess, Kirya and Kenzi,

Love forever: A Son / Brother / Father / and -Grandpa Randy-

APPRECIATION

It is with a heartfelt appreciation to my editor and advisor Jill Franklin Pugh, whom without her enduring patience, late night and early hours; coping with my constant changes and ever flowing ideas, and turning my ramblings into a coherent text, it would be a total mess of words. She is truly a Saint!

THANK YOU, JILL

Table Of Contents

Forward......................
Appreciation.................
Table of Contents ....
Dedication ....

Chapter 1
G'pa Randy Babysitting the Grandchildren
Chapter 2
The Story Continues One Cousin Less
Chapter 3
In the Boys' Bedroom
Chapter 4
The Lord's Prayer
Chapter 5
Sharing Reading the Bible
Chapter 6
The Gifted Question
Chapter 7
Explaining the Trinity
Chapter 8
"ART"
Chapter 9
Whose Imagination?
Chapter 10
 Give Us this Day

Chapter 11
 Forgive Us
Chapter 12
Another Rabbit Trail
Chapter 13
The Old Man
Chapter 14
Trespassing
Chapter 15
 Life Happens
Chapter 16
Starting to Wrap It Up
Chapter 17
 Deliver Us from the Evil One
Chapter 18
Ending the Lesson
A Note to the Readers
A Grandfathers Prayer

DEDICATION

The Holy Spirit
8 wonderful grandchildren
And any future grandchildren

Our most Holy Spirit for the inspiration of the idea of the play of the same title as this book, while riding my bike on the K.A.T.Y Trail in St. Charles, Mo. one summer day in 2006.

The original play **"The Lord's Prayer"** was written with my children as the main characters. Then, as I almost completed the play, once again riding my bike on what I called the world's largest prayer closet, The Holy Spirit told me to make the play into a children's book. However, I could not release it until my oldest grandson, Kaden, turned 10 in August of 2010. This seemed like a strange request at first, but I agreed.

Now I know why, for God knew that Kirya, my only granddaughter, and Kai, my youngest grandson, were yet to enter this world. Since this work was completed, there are 4 others now in this world. Grayson, Kenzi, Maddox, and Garrett.

CHAPTER 1
G'pa Randy Babysitting the Grandchildren

Babysitting the grandchildren could sometimes be a question as to who was watching whom—Grandpa Randy watching Kaden, Ryan, Kirya, and Kai, or just the opposite, especially when it comes time to tuck them into bed. Kaden, being the oldest of the grandchildren and not wanting to go to bed, knows the best way to get to stay up later is to just ask Grandpa to tell one of his stories, especially ones of when he was a kid. Of course, these are stories they have heard many times over, but it accomplished the goal of not going to bed on time.

"Grandpa, tell us a story," *Kaden, age 10, says.*

"Yeah, Yeah," *echoed Ryan, all of 7, and Kirya, in her best two-year-old jabbers.*

I think babies understand the gift of tongues better than adults. I just keep forgetting to pray for the gift of interpretation. Lord knows the times I could use the gift of understanding when talking on the phone to my two-year-old granddaughter!

Then the frustrating part for the both of us is me not knowing what they want, while they do! Then there is baby Kai, just completing his 1st year of life outside of his mother's tummy, sitting in his comfy chair as content as anyone could ever hope to be.

Grandpa looks at the clock and then at his grandkids. Kirya is sitting on his lap as Kaden, being tall for his age, is standing beside him. Ryan is sitting on the arm of the chair. The boys, knowing that this is supposed to be the hug, kiss and off-to-bed moment, use this time to teach their little cousins a new trick—how to stay up later when Grandpa Randy knows it's time for bed.

Grandpa says, **"It's way past your bedtime, kiddos. Your mother gets mad at me if I keep you up too late, and you**

know how your mother can get if you don't get up on time. Grandpa gets into BIG, BIG trouble."

All four kids and Grandpa begin to laugh. Even baby Kai is all smiles, as he almost always seems to be.

Kai is one of those once–in-a-lifetime babies, always smiling and having the best mellow temperament, the kind parents pray to get for their first-born. Then again maybe he is just like his daddy.

Kirya, being the only girl of the four grandkids, looks up at grandpa with that girlish smile and those BIG blue eyes and says in that heart -melting best two –year-old voice, **"Jus one, Ganpa, pease!"** *(She reminds grandpa of her mother at her age) Now how could a grandpa resist that smile and those sparkling blue eyes?*

Kaden and Ryan just smile as if to give each other an imaginary high-five, for they knew how to use their secret weapon against their grandfather— their little cousin's smile.

"Oh, just one, Grandpa. Mom won't care, just one?" *plead all three kids, as kids know how to do. Kai was in his own little happy world, loving all the attention he was getting from his grandpa and his cousins.*

"Well…maybe just one," *said Grandpa.*

Grandpa knows that Kirya won't last long and that Ryan won't be far behind, and baby Kai is pretty much already in la-la land, content where he is. Grandpa Randy also knows Kaden will be up for the duration, so he begins to tell a story that they have never heard before.

Grandpa begins, **"I remember as a young boy…About your age, Kaden, I was attending a football game with my father…Your Great-Grandpa "Snaggs." He used to keep the score during the home town football games, and I would be running around playing.**

After the game, my dad would take the press box equipment back to the coaches' office in the locker room. Now and then, I would get to go with him, and while he was putting away the equipment, I would snoop around and try to see those giant football players. I knew I was

going to be one someday, even though I was always small for my size, my heart was huge.

(Grandpa Randy did, indeed, become a football player and was the starting wide receiver for the 1969 MO. State Football Championship Class AA football team. He also went on to play college football with the #1 in the nation Jr. College football team in Miami, Oklahoma.)

Your Great-Grandfather "Snaggs" was a full-time army man and his office was in the same building as the high school gym. He always had coffee on in his office for all the PE teachers and coaches. His being athletic made it easier to be good friends with the coaches and their families, so I grew up knowing all the coaches and their kids as family friends and not just as teachers and coaches. This one night seemed to be somewhat special to me, even as a 10-year-old. This was an event that was embedded in my memory bank forever. You know, one those spine-chilling, goose-bump memories."

"What's moose-mump-ories?" *Kirya chimed in. Grandpa and the boys begin to laugh as he puts his arm around his granddaughter.*

"Not moose-mump-ories, young lady," *hugging her.* **"It's goose-bump memories. You know, those little bumps that get on your arms when you have a special event happen to you?"** *Grandpa looks at little Kirya and smiles.* **"Well, you will someday, Little Lady."**

"OK, Ganpa, "I'll have some moose mump ories someday," *Kirya said, smiling. Kaden and Ryan are used to their little cousin getting the most attention since they are brothers and they only get to see their cousin on holidays. Kaden and Ryan live in Aurora, Mo., and Kirya lives in Owego, NY, with her mom and dad. Cousin Kai is closer, in Springfield, Mo. That is a long way off for both boys and Grandpa, so Kirya pretty much has everyone's attention when they come home for the holidays or summer vacations.*

"OK, where was I?" *asked Grandpa.*

"Talking about football," *Ryan replies.*

"**Oh yeah, that night was a special night for me, a moment that gave me some moose mump ories,**" laughs Grandpa, Kaden, and Ryan. "**I remember standing in the hallway trying to get a good look at some of those Big Boy Football players. Then, after the coach gave them a pep talk and they counted down the score—that's what they did when they won a game,**" *as he looks at Kaden and Ryan,* "**I was a little shocked at what I saw and heard next.**"

"**What was that?**" *Kaden asks.*

"**You know what you do every night before you go to bed?**" *Grandpa says to Kaden and Ryan.*

"**Wash our face and hands and brush our teeth?**" *the boys said together.*

"**That too,**" *said Grandpa,* "**but what else do you do after that boys, just before you get into bed?**"

"**I know!**", *yells Ryan.*

"**And what's the answer, Ryan?**" *Grandpa says, looking at Ryan and then looking at Kaden.*

"**We say our prayers!**"

"**That's right,**" answered Grandpa.

Then Grandpa notices little Kirya is beginning to slowly start slipping into Sandman Land.

"**And before you say your prayers, you kneel down with Mom and Dad, right?**" **The boys nod their heads in agreement while Kirya nods her head off to sleep.**

"**OK, boys, I tell you what,**" whispers Grandpa. "**You go wash your face and hands. And don't forget to brush your teeth. I'll put Kirya to bed and then come back, and I'll finish my story… That is if you boys think you can stay awake?**"

Kaden and Ryan jump down off their perches and start running toward their bathroom, saying, "**OK, Grandpa, we'll be right back.**"

So, Grandpa picks up his little princess, Kirya, as he did with her mother when she was her age, and kisses her on the forehead. Just before putting her to bed, holds her up toward

Heaven and prays that Jesus will fill her with HIS Holy Spirit, and he thanks Him for allowing him to be her mother's daddy and now her granddaddy. He did the same with Kai's daddy and Kaden and Ryan's mother. This is always one of the most special times of Grandpa Randy's life, praying for and with his children before they go to bed, and now he gets to do it with his grandkids. God does answer prayers, and nothing is impossible with Him.

After returning to his chair, Kaden and Ryan's footsteps are right behind him.

CHAPTER 2
The Story Continues, One Cousin Less

"OK, Grandpa, tell us about your moose mump ories," *Kaden says as Ryan begins to get more comfortable on Grandpa's lap. Big ole' Kaden, in a chair, crowds up as close as he can to the action, for one talent Grandpa has is telling a good story.*

"OK, but first let me check behind those ears and inspect those hands and teeth." *They both lean into Grandpa so he can check behind their ears, then hold out their hands and turn them over as they look up to him and give a big, toothy smile.* **"OK, you both pass inspection, now let's get back to my story; where was I?"** *Grandpa asks again.*

"You are so forgetful, Grandpa," *says Kaden.* **"You were telling us about what the football players were doing after the coaches talked to them and counted down the score."**

"Yeah," adds Ryan, as though he has remembered every word.

It isn't a surprise to Grandpa Randy that Kaden remembers every word, for he has upgraded to the "gifted" program at his school and Ryan is just starting school. It is a proud, button-busting moment for Grandpa Randy, knowing his grandson has inherited HIS brains. ☺

"Just like you boys do every night before going to bed, all the football players took a knee. Yes, they knelt in dirty football uniforms and pads as if they were going to pray, but instead, —I was really surprised what they did next.

"What did they do, Grandpa?" *Ryan asks.* **"Quiet, Ryan, let Grandpa finish his story,"** *big brother, Kaden, says, nudging his little brother.*

"I just wanted to know," *Ryan says as he looks at his older brother. Ryan, not caring for his big brother's nudging, does some nudging of his own and if not for grandpa catching Kaden, he might have fallen off his chair.*

"Whoa there, Kaden," *Grandpa says, reaching out an arm to catch him from falling.* **"OK, boys let's settle down and listen."**

"OK, grandpa," *both boys said together.*

"The talk by the coach was not what I remembered, but what will FOREVER be a goose bump moment . . ."

"Don't you mean a moose mump ories?" *Kaden blurts out as they all laugh.*

"Yes, a moose mump ories moment," *says* Grandpa, chuckling to himself. **"When the coach finished his talk, he asked a senior member of the squad to lead them all in "The Lord's Prayer". This was not such a big deal during the early 1960s, for you see, prayer was still allowed and even encouraged in the public schools. However, it was the way this captain led the prayer. They didn't say it... They SANG it,"** *Grandpa says in his serious voice, as he looks at both grandsons.*

"In a surprisingly mature, deeper bass voice than what you would expect from a senior in high school, he, and the entire football team, and coaches began to SING "The Lord's Prayer." You could hear the members of the glee club who also played football above all others, and their harmony was bone chilling. Yes, even to this day I still get 'moose mumps' just thinking about it."

Kaden and Ryan are both listening "real close" to Grandpa's story.

"I saw and heard this locker room with half of the players out of shoulder pads and in sweaty T-shirts, and some still in full uniform. ALL were kneeling in reverence to this prayer, and I heard the most beautiful song you

ever could imagine: men singing, "The Lord's Prayer."

Grandpa Randy stops to think for a moment when Ryan is noticeably starting to follow his little cousin to Sandman Land. Grandpa asks Ryan if he is getting sleepy, but he sits up like a big boy and is not about to lose the battle to stay awake.

"What's "The Lord's Prayer"? *Kaden asks.*

"It's the prayer Jesus taught His disciples and a lot of people who were gathered around him when he was still on Earth teaching, preaching and healing people," *Grandpa adds.* **"The followers of Jesus came and asked Him if He would teach them to pray."** *Grandpa stops his story.* ***"I tell you what, gentlemen,"*** *he says, seeing Ryan fading fast.* **"What do you think about us going into your bedroom to finish the story?"**

Kaden, seeing his little brother's eyes getting very heavy, agrees, saying, **"That would be a good idea."**

So, Grandpa Randy nudges up Ryan, and with Kaden leading the way, they head off to the boys' bedroom. Grandpa Randy tucks Ryan in next to his cousin, Kirya, and gives him a hug and kiss, and tells him he loves him, and to listen and he'll finish the story. Little Kai has long ago lingered into a deep sleep in his portable sleeper, now placed beside his two sleepyhead cousins.

CHAPTER 3
In the Boys' Bedroom

Kaden now has Grandpa's sole attention as they both sit on his bed and Grandpa Randy begins to teach his grandson about **"The Lord's Prayer."**

This is a special moment for them both, but especially for Grandpa Randy. As he is getting Kaden ready to tuck into bed, He is having a couple of flashback memories of when Kaden was born. Grandpa Randy was the first one in the family to hold him…of course that was after the doctors, nurses, mom, and dad had their turns. Before handing baby Kaden to his Grandmother Deborah, he lifted him up toward Heaven and asked God to bless him. Grandpa Randy remembers the first six months of young Kaden's life.

At that time, he only lived two miles from the new family and at least a couple of days a week could walk to their house and babysit with baby Kaden while his mother could either get some sleep or catch up on some house work. Why sometimes he would spend the night with them while Kaden's daddy was out of town training for his auto parts store manager's position. He was a hard worker and led by example. He totally turned at least three businesses from losing stores into very profitable ones.

There was one night that Grandpa spent the night, and was so in love with his new grandson, that he just couldn't bear to put him in his baby bed to sleep. He pulled all the cushions and pillows from the couch and chairs, and he laid them down next to the couch where he slept (just in case baby Kaden rolled off in the night.) He then laid down to sleep, with

Kaden sleeping on his soft belly and chest. They both fell fast asleep, but Grandpa Randy would sleep most of the time with one eye open to make sure Kaden didn't roll off the couch. Well, this night, Grandpa had both eyes go to sleep at the same time and, sure enough, he took a deep breath and baby Kaden rolled right off his belly and onto the cushions beside the couch. However, when Kaden made his first move, Grandpa Randy, being a light sleeper, was quick to react. By the time Kaden had hit the cushions beside the couch, he already had his hands on him and caught him on the first bounce. Ok, so it wasn't on the first bounce. Kaden did hit the cushions but never batted an eye or woke up. Grandpa Randy just picked him up, placed him between the back of the couch and himself, and went back to sleep...yes, but this time, with only one eye at a time. No wonder this was such a special bedtime moment... there just seemed to be that special connection between the two of them.

"OK, big guy," **Grandpa Randy says to Kaden. "Let's finish the story, for I was just about your age when this all took place."**

Kaden looks at his grandpa and asks, **"Grandpa, why is it called "The Lord's Prayer?"**

This question comes as no surprise to Grandpa R, for although he knows Kaden has learned and said this prayer before becoming a "King's Kid" at an early age, his interest is more intense as if there are still missing blanks in his understanding.

Grandpa replies, **"Because it was the prayer Jesus taught to his disciples and all the people gathered around him."**

"Can you teach me "The Lord's Prayer" too, Grandpa?" *Kaden asks.*

"Hey, K-man," *as Grandpa Randy often calls Kaden.* **"Why don't we make this your bedtime prayer tonight, OK?"**

"Good idea, Grandpa R," *Kaden replies.*

"Yes, Kaden, I think maybe you are old enough to learn "The Lord's Prayer."

CHAPTER 4
"The Lord's Prayer"

*Both are sitting on the side of Kaden's bed. Grandpa Randy reaches for Kaden's children's Bible and begins to turn the pages until he comes to Matthew, Chapter 6, **verse 9.** He looks at Kaden and points to the scripture.*

He begins to explain. **"Kaden, this is a time when Jesus was just beginning His ministry as an adult. People from all over the country had heard of the miracles that Jesus had been accomplishing, like healing the sick, making blind eyes see, and crippled people walk again. So just think, if you heard of someone doing that today, you'd want to see this man, Jesus, for yourself, wouldn't you?"**

Grandpa waits for Kaden's answer as he looks over to Ryan's bed and notices he has already fallen fast asleep.

"No kidding!" *Kaden chimes in, as he was reminded of how Grandpa Randy has the talent to make stories come alive by using his hands, eyes, and arm gestures and many funny voices to demonstrate his explanation.*

Grandpa begins to read from Kaden's Bible. **"Jesus saw a huge crowd gathering toward Him, he chose a spot on the side of a hill, high up with His disciples beside Him, and he began to teach them. Kaden, Jesus taught many wonderful ways we are supposed to live. Many of those ways people today have forgotten."**

"Like what ways, Grandpa?" *Kaden's eyes grow big, and he is all ears.*

"For example, just before he started the lesson on "The Lord's Prayer," he was teaching about humility." *Grandpa Randy is beginning to teach his grandson Kaden about Jesus.*

"Hu Mil La DE?" *Kaden questions?*

Grandpa sounds out the word **"Humility"** *very slowly.* *"Hu Mil La T," Grandpa says.* **"That's when Jesus was teaching the crowds and His disciples that when they do a good deed—"** *Grandpa hesitates for a second thinking of an example Kaden will understand.* **"Like the time when you gave your favorite Star Wars toy to Ryan without asking or telling your mom or dad what you had done…You did it in a secret way that only God and Ryan knew."** *Grandpa looks to see his grandson's face, making sure he understands his message. Kaden has that surprised, curious look in his eyes as if he wants to ask how, if only God knows that, did Grandpa find out? But Grandpa R doesn't give him the chance to ask. He just continues to teach.*

"That's what Jesus was talking about, doing something without bragging about it. Like you did, Kaden. I know it meant a lot to you to give up your favorite toy, but you did a good thing, Grandson…But that's a different lesson for another night. Tonight, we are going to look at the lesson Jesus gave about how to Pray.

CHAPTER 5
Sharing Reading the Bible

Grandpa Randy redirects Kaden's attention back to the Bible and begins reading. **"Kaden, I'll read this one line after another, and you repeat the line after me. You will get a better feeling on how the prayer goes, OK?"** *He waits for Kaden to respond.*

"Uh…OK, Grandpa," *Kaden says quickly, although wondering just where Grandpa R is going with this, still wide awake and anxious to learn.*

Grandpa R thinks to himself how much his grandson shares his love for learning, always eager to jump at a chance to learn something new…an inborn love of learning that naturally goes with a love of teaching. It's in the DNA.

Grandpa R then begins to read again.

"Matt: 6:9: 'This, then, is how you should pray: 'Our Father who art in heaven, hallowed be thy name.'"

He pauses and waits for Kaden to repeat after reading each line and, to his surprise, this is what he has heard:

"My grandfather, who paints pictures of Heaven, how many know his name?"

Grandpa R jerks his head back as if hit with a sudden, startling, "DID YOU SEE THAT?" kind of expression, and looks at his grandson like "Where did that come from?"

"What did you just say?"

"My grandfather, who paints pictures of Heaven, how many know his name?" *Kaden repeats what his 10-year-old* *ears thought they heard and processed its meaning.* **"How did you get that from what I just read… 'Our Father who art in Heaven, Hallowed be thy name?'"**

Without hesitation, Kaden begins to explain. **"Well, you said Our Father…And you're the only father I know in this room… And except for my other grandfather and great grandfather, "Snaggs,"** *Kaden says in a matter-of-fact voice,* **"… you're my only grandfather who draws and paints pictures of clouds… And I don't know how many know your name?"**

"Ah, now, it all begins to make sense," *Grandpa R says.*

Sometimes when I try to teach someone else something I know, like how to hit a baseball or how to correctly throw one—something I've been doing all my life—I forget it's new to them. I forget that they don't have all the details in their head like I do, so I must slow down, regroup and start again, this time with the basics.

"OK…well that's a new one on me," *says Grandpa Randy, still in a little-surprised voice.* **"Let me explain in a little more detail, Grandson,"** *he says, reassuring Kaden his answer is OK.* **"In this instance, Jesus was talking about our Heavenly Father…He was praying to His Father, who still lives in Heaven….is that a little clearer, Kaden?"** *Grandpa Randy asks.*

"Yep!" *says Kaden.* **"God is our Heavenly Father, right, Grandpa?"**

Grandpa Randy is amazed at Kaden's understanding. Maybe he really is ready to learn "The **Lord's Prayer,"** *he thinks to himself.* **"And another word for Hallowed is……honored, a Holy name above any other name in Heaven or Earth."** *Grandpa Randy can see Kaden is deep in thought and patiently waits for his response.*

"Grandpa?" *Kaden asks in a slow, thoughtful manner,* **"Doesn't that mean Jesus and our Heavenly Father were the same person? How could Jesus be praying to himself?"**

Shocked, Grandpa says, **"WHOA, K, that's a question most adults don't even think of and that's another lesson for another time, but I will try to make the best brief explanation I can, although that will be a mighty tall challenge."** *Grandpa Randy was surprised… OK, shocked when Kaden asked him to explain "The Lord's Prayer", and now this was getting deep fast. You never think kids this young ever listen to a word you, or the Sunday school teacher, or preacher says, but then my kids have always been intelligent, deep thinkers and have often caught me off guard with some of the most interesting questions.* **"Whoa, partner! When did you get so smart on your ole grandpa?"**

"Well, Grandpa, you know I am in the gifted class at school, don't you?" *Kaden asks, looking up to his Grandpa Randy and waiting for an answer.*

"Yes, I do, Kaden, and I must say I am a PROUD grandpa knowing that I have at least one grandson who got his grandpa's smarts, HA! HA! HA!" *He gave his grandson a great big hug and a hearty laugh!*

"But let me see if I can answer that gifted question," *replies Grandpa Randy.*

CHAPTER 6
The Gifted Question

"Kaden," *Grandpa says in a more serious voice, changing the mood of the moment,* **"there are four things I have learned to pray for every day. These four are taught throughout the Bible, and are in the book of Proverbs and 1st Corinthians 12, as gifts of the Holy Spirit."** *He stops and turns the pages of Kaden's Bible as he catches his breath.*

"What are you looking up, Grandpa?" *Kaden asks. He knows that when Grandpa Randy starts teaching something, you'd better have your fast-listening ears on, and you don't have much of a chance to talk.*

"Here it is. Proverbs chapter 1: 2," *Grandpa says as if speaking to himself.*

<u>**'Proverbs 1:2** **to know Wisdom and Instruction; to Discern the words of Understanding'**</u> **What this is talking about, Kaden, is that we should seek and pray for these four gifts every day:**

1. To seek after God's Wisdom
2. To seek after God's Knowledge
3. To seek after God's Understanding
4. To seek after God's Discernment

Grandpa Randy stops for a minute when he notices a confused look on his grandson's face. **"OK, Kaden, I see I'm getting a little TOO gifted for a 10-year-old, right?"** *He says, giving Kaden a little hug.*

"W E L L! I do understand about understanding knowledge, I have to understand my homework, you know, or I wouldn't make good grades," *Kaden replies,* **uncertain of his answer.**

CHAPTER 7
Explaining the Trinity

"All right, Sport, I'm going to draw you a picture, and you just remember in that gifted mind of yours that when you get a little older and ready for this, the Holy Spirit will bring it back to your memory…OK?"

Grandpa Randy says, hoping he isn't getting TOO much over his head. He thinks to himself, "Lord, help me explain this to Kaden, so he will get a better understanding of who you are." I guess I'm going to see just how well those prayers are answered as I try to explain to a 10-year-old about the understanding of the Holy Trinity.

"Got it, Grandpa R, I'm all tuned in…go for it GR," *Kaden says as he is putting his hands up to his ears like he is tuning in a radio or a DVD player.*

"Kaden, let me see if I can make this a little less complicated…. and by the way, that was a very adult question you just asked. There are many grown-ups still looking for an answer to that. I am not saying that I have the perfect answer, but I will do my best, as I have come to understand the mystery of the Trinity and OUR FATHER."

Grandpa Randy begins to draw a line down the middle of the dry erase board and about four inches from the top, he draws another line across the board. He then spells out in a vertical row in column one.

Understand The Holy Spirit

Trinity   3 in 1   Tri-Unity

1.God the Father	1.Our Mind
(Likeness / Emotions)	(Will and Emotions)
2.God the Son	2.Our Body
(God in flesh / Body)	(Flesh Suit We Live In)
3.God the Holy Spirit	3.Our Spirit
(Breath of God)	(Life Within Us)

1. God the Father-made in His likeness and emotions

2. God the Son –God came to Earth in the Flesh

3. God the Holy Spirit –the breath of God is Life

On the other side, he begins to do the same format, only he writes:

1.   Mind – Will and Emotions

2.   Body – Our flesh suit

3.   Spirit – Life within us, breath of God

"Kaden, as I understand from the book of Genesis 1:26 it said, 'Then God said, 'Let us make man in our image, in our likeness…'"

Kaden notices that anytime Grandpa Randy starts talking about God and reading the Bible, all joking and playing are put aside. Grandpa Randy is very serious when he is talking about God, Jesus, and the Holy Spirit. This makes him listen even more closely.

"He was referring to US as Our Heavenly Father, His Son (Jesus), and His Holy Spirit, all three in one and THEY created us in THEIR IMAGE and LIKENESS." *Grandpa Randy is pointing to the drawing he has made.* **"To me, this means, that although there are three in one, the Holy Trinity,"** *Now pointing to the bottom part of the drawing.* **"We are a TRI-UNITY of Body, Mind, and Spirit. We are three**

parts as well but in one body. Is this making any sense, **Big Guy?"** *He waits for Kaden to approve.*

"I can see it more clearly by the picture you just drew, but..." *Kaden says in a puzzling tone of voice and stops as if he is thinking of what to say next, but Grandpa Randy doesn't wait for his next thought, seeing Kaden is trying to understand.*

"It's like this, K-man, our body is created in the Holy Trinity's image," *Grandpa points to the body part of the drawing,* **"and our mind and spirit are in their likeness."** *Grandpa points to the other parts of the chart.* "And, **since Adam was the first man to be created, that makes God the father of all mankind, and we fit in that category, right, Bucko?"** *By this time Kaden is starting to realize that Grandpa is doing as he does so many times when telling a story or teaching about Jesus. If you ask him a question, he gets off the subject and on to another one so quickly.*

"Whatever you say, Grandpa R...I believe you when you teach me about God and the Bible, I just don't always understand what you're saying."

"I did it again for the Umpteenth time, didn't I, K-man?", *he says.* **He realizes about the same time** *that he has gotten off the subject, AGAIN!* **"Just remember this drawing, and when you get a little older, the Holy Spirit will help you remember what I have taught, and HE will give you the understanding. OK? Are we straight for now?"** *Kaden smiles and nods in agreement, giving his grandpa R a big hug.*

"Let's get back to the Our Father who ART in Heaven."

CHAPTER 8
"ART"

Kaden speaks up before Grandpa R can start again. **"Art is when you draw something, right? And you are always drawing or painting, so I just thought you were doing a picture of Heaven."**

Looking surprised, Grandpa continues, **"OK, so now I understand your thinking, and I can be a bit 'hallow once in a while, right K-man?"**

Kaden just grins really BIG!

"I'll try to make things a little easier from now on...but the next word is HALLOWED and not any resemblance of Halloween...OK"?

Kaden sighs and takes a deep breath as he knows just to nod and be ready for the next round of Grandpa R.

"The word Hallowed here means a VERY HOLY Name...A name to honor, respect and not to use in every sentence or bad language as you hear so many people do today. The name JESUS, God, and Holy Spirit, when understood correctly, will be spoken with a much-respected understanding...in fact, K-man, in the book of Deuteronomy, it states in the second of the 10 commandments...Remember we studied the 10 commandments in one of your Sunday school lessons?" *He waits for his grandson to give a response.*

"Uh...I think so," *Kaden quickly responds before Grandpa R has a chance to ask another question.* **"Yeah, I remember**

part of it. **Mom is always reminding me of the part where it says to obey your parents,"** *Kaden adds as his grandpa is looking up another scripture.*

"As I was saying," *Grandpa begins,* **"In Deuteronomy 5:11, 'Thou shalt not take the name of the LORD thy God in vain: for the LORD will not hold him guiltless that taketh his name in vain.' That, my grandson, is a very serious commandment, we really need to remember God's not kidding when he says NOT to take His name in vain—which means unless you are witnessing, praying, preaching, or teaching about Jesus, we should not be uttering His name. It's just not right. In fact, God commands it!"**

Kaden knows when Grandpa R only says, "GRANDSON" without a smile, or adding the K with it, he is serious and whomever he is teaching had better be listening well. Kaden grabs his grandpa's arm and looks up at him saying, **"OK... see if I got it...When we pray 'Our Father' we are talking to God, Our Father of all people, and He lives in Heaven, and His name is VERY Holy...right? And we are not to use His name unless we are telling people about Jesus, praying, preaching, or teaching someone about Him. Is that correct?"**

(Grandpa R and grandson exchange a "high five.")

"Give me five, K-man! That's a GOOD explanation. I'm very proud of you. Now I know why you advanced to the gifted program?"

Grandpa R was smiling again, and Kaden knows he has, once again, made his grandpa proud of him but takes a deep sigh knowing there was still yet more to come.

"Thanks, Grandpa, now try staying on the subject, OK? I don't have all night," *Kaden quickly adds, with a great BIG smile!*

"Agreed. Now let's get on with the 'LORD'S PRAYER.'" *Grandpa R says with a BIGGER smile. They both sit back on the bed next to each other, in a more relaxed position. Grandpa R gives him a left arm hug and then picks up the Bible and begins teaching.* **"OK, we have covered 'Our**

Father who art in heaven, hallowed be thy name.' Next is 'Thy Kingdom come, Thy will be done, on Earth as it is in Heaven.'"

CHAPTER 9
Taking Turns Reading

Grandfather raises his hand and then says :

"Wait, before you say a word, I think it would be a good idea for you to actually see the words, rather than to leave it to your overactive imagination. I have no idea who you might have received that from—must have been your mother."

(They look at each other and laugh out loud as if they both really know from whom he received his imagination. Grandpa Randy redirects his grandson's eyes to the correct line in the Bible and says...) **"Uh…here it is, OK, you read this aloud to me."**

(Kaden starts re-reading at the beginning, in a mid-tone range, and when he comes to the next line, he speaks in a louder voice.) **"Our Father, who art in Heaven, hallowed be thy name…Thy kingdom come, Thy will be done, on Earth as it is in Heaven… OK, Grandpa, I have heard this prayer in church many times but the words never really seem to mean anything. What does 'Thy Kingdom come, Thy will be done mean?"**

Taking a deep breath, Grandpa snuggles closer to Kaden so they can both read out of the same Bible.

"Thy Kingdom come" …The best I can explain it is that from the beginning of Jesus' ministry, He was always trying to teach and prepare the people. He was preparing

even for us who were born much later, for when He would return to Earth…for when we are in the presence of the Holy Spirit, we are in the midst of the Kingdom of God."

(Interrupting, Kaden says…) "But, Grandpa, doesn't Jesus live in our hearts when we get saved and ask Him to come live inside us? This is all confusing."

Grandpa R is beginning to think that this is turning into a very long bedtime story, but an excellent teachable moment.

"You know, you're right. Jesus, the Holy Spirit, and God the Father, does live in your Spiritual heart and not your Thumper heart. "I sometimes guess the meaning of the scriptures can seem confusing. That's why God told us that if we really work hard at finding Him with ALL our Heart, ALL our mind, and ALL our Spirit, we will find Him. Sometimes, it is just easier to sit in a pew in church and listen to the preacher talk, instead of really getting in and studying the Holy Scriptures for ourselves."

"So, if Jesus, the Holy Spirit, and God Our Father, live in our spiritual hearts, and, also, in Heaven, then heaven must live inside of us, too," Kaden says. "Right?"

Grandpa is blown away at the depth of Kaden's thinking and yet very proud at the same time, for most 10-year-olds are not thinking at this level. **"That's a good way to understand it, and you will always gain just a little more understanding the more you study God's word. The part of 'Thy will be done, on Earth, as it is in Heaven' reminds me of the time Jesus was in the Garden praying before He was betrayed and turned over for crucifixion. You know, Kaden, Jesus could have, at any second, just called out to Heaven and 12,000 Angels would have come and rescued Him from all the pain and suffering He was about to endure. But he didn't. He prayed to His Father in Heaven and said, 'Not my will but yours be done.' Matt 26:39 "So, even though Jesus was still on Earth, He was willing to do what His Father, who is in Heaven, wanted, and not what we on Earth most often wanted. Is this making any sense at all, K?"**

"Wellllll…more so than just reading the words or hearing people say them."

"Just remember this lesson and where to go find the answers. Know where the scripture is and, when you get older, you will understand it even better. Remember, knowing where to go to find the answers is just as important as just memorizing a bunch of words. OK, where were we? Here it is, are you ready to read or use that imagination of yours?"

CHAPTER 10
Give Us This Day

"I'll read, 'Our Father who art in Heaven, Hallowed be thy name. Thy Kingdom come, Thy will be done, on Earth as it is in Heaven.' Here we are... 'Give us this day our daily bread...'"

"Daily Bread?' Do we have to eat bread every day? Oh boy, I love bread!"

"ME, TOO! Bread is one of my favorite meals." (They both laugh.) However, I don't think this is exactly talking about dinner rolls. It means more like when Moses led the Israelites out of Egypt into the desert on their way to the Promised Land. They didn't have any grocery stores to buy food as they traveled across the desert, and even though they kept complaining, God still, gave them brand new food to eat every day, except for Saturdays when He gave them enough for two days so they wouldn't have to work on the Sabbath. Not one day did all the millions of people ever go hungry. The food God provided for them was called 'manna.' It was sort of like our bread only a whole lot healthier. When we say provide for us our 'daily bread' we really mean our daily NEEDS, not our wants or greed. And I've had a few days when I was happy to just have some bread in the house."

Kaden's eyes widen and his mouth is open as wide as a cave door. Panicked, he exclaims, "Does that mean no more Christmas gifts or birthday gifts?"

Grandpa gives a reassuring hug and says, **"No! No! Kaden. Surprises are a good thing now and then. God even gave us His best gift when He gave us Jesus, His only Son, so that whosoever would believe in Him SHOULD NOT perish. (John 3:16), so Gifts are a GOOD THING!"**

Fluffing his pillow and putting it behind his head, Kaden gives a sigh of relief. **"Geezer Louiezzzer, that was a close one…. What's next? …your turn to read, Grandpa."**

(Turning back to the open pages, Grandpa uses his right index finger to look for the spot where they left off.) **"I was wondering if I was going to get a turn. Here we are…back on the road again. Oh, this one is a tough one, K-man… of all the lessons in life, I think this is one of the hardest I have had to work on. Ouch! It even hurts sometimes to just read it."**

CHAPTER 11
"Forgive Us"

"You want me to read it for you?"

"No," laughs Grandpa, **"that would be taking the easy way out...I guess I needed this lesson more than you... OK, here goes. 'And forgive us our debts (trespasses) AS we forgive our debtors.'"**

"So why is that so hard, G'pa?"

"Well, K-man, when you really stop to think about what Jesus is saying...I mean really understand it...well...It means that Jesus will only forgive us of our wrong doing to the degree that we forgive others who do us wrong."

"WHAAAAT? I just figured all we had to do was just ask for forgiveness, and our SIN board was wiped clean, *exclaims Kaden."*

"That is true for our Salvation, K-man, when we ask Jesus to forgive us our sins and come live in our newly cleaned spiritual heart. Unfortunately, most people think just asking to be forgiven is the EASY BUTTON and ticket to Heaven, and they don't read the few verses below the teaching of "The Lord's Prayer" ... Let's just look a little closer at what Jesus taught his disciples." *(Turning to the book of Matthew, chapter 6: 14-15), G'pa uses his index finger, starting at the top of Matthew 6: and acting if he is skimming down the page, to find this scripture.)* **"Remember, Kaden...this is still JESUS teaching on the hillside... But this is what the Apostles understood to hear. It sure**

makes one stop to think a lot more about just forgiving from our head instead of our heart. For it's not the words we say that count...it's the truth of how we feel in our heart that concerns OUR FATHER. If you don't learn anything else from this lesson on how to pray...PLEASE! Learn how to forgive from your heart...OK, Grandson?" Remember these are the words of JESUS. Matt: 6: 14 "for if ye forgive men their trespasses, your heavenly Father will also forgive you: 15 but if ye forgive not men their trespasses, neither will your Father forgive your trespasses." *(Grandpa R hesitates and then says with mild surprise, pointing to the reference with his right index finger and giving his grandson a slight left elbow to get his attention.)* "Here, look at this reference to Matthew 18:35."

"So likewise shall my heavenly Father do also unto you, if you from your HEARTS forgive not every one his brother and their trespasses."

"I didn't know Jesus was so serious about the forgiving part," *Kaden says.* "It really must be important."

"I think it may be more than just important. I think it's more of a command. Kind of like Jesus is saying, "My way or the highway, Jack. If I'm going to have to go through what I am for your sins to be forgiven, then forgiving each other is the least you can do."

CHAPTER 12
Another Rabbit Trail

Grandpa heads down another one of his rabbit trails of memories. **"Kaden…for years as a young lad in a Catholic grade school, I was an altar boy…I was even personally requested by the Bishop, when he came for a visit to our church to say Mass during the Holy Week, to hold the big book from which he would read. After my first time, he realized I had steady hands to hold the book of prayers so he could read during Mass…just thought I'd throw that in for free…hold out your hands, Kaden, let me see if they are nervous or steady.** *Kaden holds out his hands as Grandpa R asked him to do.* **"Yeah, like a rock. No surprise to me."**

(Grandpa R takes the Bible and holds it in front of him, as he would hold it so someone else could read it...then moves it around in a playful way as to show why having a steady hand is a good thing for an altar boy. Then, placing it back on his lap, he starts to explain more...but hesitates so he can look down into Kai's traveling sleeping bed. He checks on Ryan in his bed and Kirya, fast asleep next to him, then he sits in front of Kaden as if holding the book so he can read it, as an example of how G'pa R used to do for the visiting Bishop at church.) **"I always felt a closeness to God when holding the book for the Bishop. Did you know that at one time I seriously considered going into the priesthood?"** *Then, as if talking to himself, he begins to get back on track.*

"I have recited "The Lord's Prayer" since I started first grade, but it wasn't until I started studying the Bible for myself, and not just reading it, or listening to someone else give a sermon, did I begin to understand its meaning. For me, Kaden, this woke me up in my Christian Life. I guess we all have our weaknesses, but I pray God gives me His Grace and Mercy to help me get to where I need to be. I pray the same for you every night."

"Wait a minute, G'pa…you mean you have weaknesses? I thought you were pretty tough for an old man!"

"What do you mean old man?" *(They break out laughing.)*

Kaden jumps from the bed and runs out of the room shouting, **"OK, hold your place. I gotta go to the bathroom."**

(As Kaden goes to relieve himself, Grandpa R has a flashback memory.)

Now that was a low blow! I refuse to get old! I must have been all of 57 years old and thought myself to still be in pretty good athletic form…why, just ask me. In my mind, I can still run a 100-yd dash in 10 seconds; however, my body even laughs at me. I'd be lucky to do a 100-yd dash in 30 seconds in a golf cart.

One night, a couple of years after graduating from high school and running a 10-sec 100-yd dash, a classmate and I got into a discussion…Heck, it was an argument, about being able to run the same times we did just a couple of years before in track. He was a 2-miler, what did he know about sprints? Anyway, it got down to put-up or shut-up. He had a stopwatch in his car, and we headed to the track. It was a summer evening and, at this age, I always kept my, bat, balls, golf clubs, running shoes, etc. in the trunk of my car. I came prepared for any game. We went to the track, and the best I could do was 11.5. Of course, it was in street shorts and tennis shoes…YEAH! I had to laugh about that one, too, yet in my mind, I can still run that 100-yd dash in 10 seconds. Anyway, I can still hit a slow pitch softball!

I sure miss those trying days or at least some of them. I

don't miss having to work three jobs trying to make ends meet, when the only thing that met was me, coming and going. I must have had at least two or three burnouts during the first 10 years of our family. I can remember coming in from a night shift at 5 a.m. and going to my daughter's baby bed. She must have been all of 6 months old. I'd pick her up just to hold her, rock her, and pray for her. I did the same for my children when they were born, yet they never batted an eyelash and never knew their daddy did such a thing. It had to be the rocking chair, for I know it wasn't my singing or composition of a poem of thankfulness that kept them asleep. Gee, I always thought if I had a way to record my thoughts when I first had them, I'd have written some pretty good stuff. But, as usual, by the time I finished my time with my special gift from God and put my baby down, then remembered what words of rhythm and rhyme that had just crossed my mind, the moment had passed.

I realize now that it was just a special moment between God, my child, and me, not to share for fame. Yes, a precious moment. How we, as young parents, do not realize until years later just how special those moments turn out to be.

(Grandpa pauses as he waits for his grandson to come back. He leans his head back on the headboard. When Kaden returns he hits his grandpa in the arm and tells him to wake up. They exchange playful blows with each other for his wisecrack. He then begins speaking in an exaggerated comic tone of an old, old man).

CHAPTER 13
The Old Man

"I'll tell you what, Sonny…you just put up your dukes, and I'll show you weak for an old man. Well, I'll give you the what for, you young whippersnapper!"

Kaden and Grandpa R begin to wrestle, and cackle, and snicker quietly, so as not to wake the other kids. After all, this is a special time between a grandfather and a grandson. Only the full impact of such memory-making is more for the elder than the younger; a blessed time, a special moment for sure. (Grandpa R regains his composure and redirects his grandson's attention to the Bible.)

"OK, Big Guy, any more questions before we move on to the next verse, or are you ready for some shut eye?"

"Yeah, OLD MAN, tell me, what did the prayer mean by debtors? I understand trespasses, I think. Isn't it like the signs posted when we go hunting, 'NO TRESPASSING?' We are not supposed to cross the fence?"

CHAPTER 14
Trespassing

"Yes, K, just like it, only different." *(They give each other that 'deer-in-the-headlights' look and stare at one another in a fun, surprised look.)*

"Say that again!" *Kaden exclaims.*

"You mean 'Just like it, only different?' Sounds funny, doesn't it? But it is just like "no trespassing" signs when hunting. We are not supposed to cross certain marked boundary lines, or we could get into some deep trouble with the landowner. That's why the correct thing to do is always ask permission from the owner before hunting on his property. We all have our own personal fences and boundary lines we don't allow or want anyone to cross without our permission. Sometimes WE forget to ask permission, or accidentally on purpose, or on purpose, do or say something to hurt someone's feelings, property, or private areas of their life. When we do so, we commit a trespass, then we owe a debt of forgiveness to that person. Then again, we are to forgive those who hurt our feelings, property or harm us. Debt, debtors or Trespasses all mean the same thing."

(Grandpa turns quickly to Luke 6:28 and shows him what the Bible says.) **"Let's look in Luke…say that three times fast. These, too, are the very words of Jesus in the book of Luke chapter 6:27-28. 27: 'But I say unto you which hear, love your enemies, do good to them which hate**

you, 28: Bless them that curse you, and pray for them which despitefully use you.' Perhaps that's what makes it so hard for us men because if someone tries to hurt me, I'm just as apt to punch him in the nose and then ask for his forgiveness. Perhaps we all still have some spiritual growing to do. I will love them from a distance and pray for those who intentionally want to say and spread rumors about me. That way, I won't be so apt to do something my human nature hasn't perfected yet, but that's getting off subject just a bit. Like I said, K-man, this is a hard one for me."

HARD! Well, that was the understatement of my life. Little did I know just how hard it was going to be in my future years. God really knows how to turn up the heat and, sadly to say, so does that ole devil. Looking back, (Well let's not), suffice it to say that I sure would like to have back a bunch of those immature, misspoken words that flew out of my mouth…And sometimes even to MY surprise! Personal hurt, pain, and rejection seem to bring the worst out in me, and God knows, I've had my share, and I swear, half of someone else's. I'll have to ask God when I get to Heaven if perhaps some angels went to sleep and forgot to pass a little of this pain, hurt, and rejection around. LOL!

CHAPTER 15
Life Happens

"Kaden, life happens, and along the way, we do learn to forgive, or we get bitter. Yeah! As my wise old Grandfather Haddock used to say, 'Get better or get bitter.' Sad, so many of us get bitter before we learn to get better...But God has a way to get our attention. Yeah, sooner or later. Sooner or later, we learn forgiveness, or at least we pray we do. To not forgive is unhealthy because it opens your spiritual heart to other sinful things. The Bible describes it as a cancer."

Chapter 16
Starting to Wrap It Up

(Kaden begins to show signs of getting sleepy and snuggles just a little closer to his grandpa. Grandpa puts his left arm around him, welcoming the closeness. Then he begins to close the lesson by continuing to read the next verse.)

"It's getting late, isn't it, Kaden? Your mom, dad, and aunt, and uncles will be getting home soon. Let's wrap this lesson up by reading the last part. I think that this will help you to understand it better, and won't have so many questions. I can see the day is catching up with the both of us. Verse 13… *(Grandpa reads it to himself silently as if to make sure of where he left off the last verse. He then repeats aloud…Verse 13.)* "Hmmmmm...Verse 13…I think everyone has this problem."

"What problem, Grandpa?" *(Kaden says sleeply)*

"It says 'Lead us NOT into temptation, BUT deliver us from evil.'"

"I understand the temptation part. It's hard to walk past those fresh-baked, warm double chocolate chip cookies Mom baked today, without snatching one to see if they were good enough for the rest of you guys to eat. But a little voice inside me said I'd better not, or was that Mom yelling from the other room? Hard to tell the difference." *(Both give a hardy, but sleepy, chuckle.)*

"Yeah, I know…you was just thinking of our health, right, K-Man? I know for myself, there is always something ready to test my weaknesses, every day, and a double-

dipped chocolate chip cookie would be one of them. Are there any left?" *Kaden and Grandpa Randy look at each other and laugh.*

CHAPTER 17
Deliver us from Evil

"What always seemed to catch my eye on this verse, Kaden, was the second part when Jesus said, 'BUT deliver us from evil.' It seemed to me that it was like Jesus already knew we would, at some time or another, fall to our temptations and fall into the hands of our spiritual enemies. So, he added an insurance policy at the end… 'BUT deliver us from evil" and in verses 14 and 15, to show you how important this part of the prayer is, Jesus AGAIN says, '14 For if you forgive men when they sin against you, your Heavenly Father will also forgive you. 15 but if you do not forgive men their sins, your Father will not forgive your sins.' It's as if Jesus didn't think they understood it the first time.   He was teaching them how to pray. He said it for a second time in the same lesson."

CHAPTER 18
Ending the Lesson

(By this time Kaden is beginning to fade and starting to slump over into his grandpa's lap and onto the Bible. Grandpa gently pulls him up just enough to be able to put the Bible down behind him at the foot of his bed. Grandpa Randy starts to hum the song, "The Lord's Prayer," that he heard in that football locker room years ago. As he gets up from the bed while holding on to his sleepy grandson…He turns toward the bed and repositions Kaden, so his head is on his pillow, then helps his grandson put his legs under the half-turned-down covers. As he is finishing up tucking him in, giving him a kiss on the forehead, and telling him how much he loves him, Kaden, in his last breath before the Sandman wins this battle for awake time, looks up at Grandpa Randy. He gives him a hug and says, **"Good night, Grandpa, I love you, too, and thanks for letting me stay up and learn about "The Lord's Prayer."**

With tears in his eyes, Grandpa begins saying **"The Lord's Prayer."** *As Grandpa Randy gives each one of his blessed grandchildren a kiss and says a prayer over each one, he turns out the lights and makes sure the night light is on before heading back to the other room. He is close by so he can hear the babies should they awaken.*

He quietly begins to sing **"The Lord's Prayer"** *out loud, as he reaches that comfy recliner where he started the night. He then begins to sing a little louder in a spirit of worship and prayer.*

"For Thine is the Kingdom and the Power and the Glory

forever! Aaaaaaaaamen~!" (Then repeats.) "For Thine is the Kingdom and the Power and the Glory forever! Aaaaaaaaamen~!

He then remembers when it was that he first began to write this book. He recalls the Holy Spirit telling him not to release it until Kaden was 10 years or older. Now he knows why for Kirya and Kai had not yet been born.

He needed to revise this book, and with happiness, wondered if maybe there were any more grandchildren in the making. Yes, there were 4 more Grandkids yet to come.

A NOTE TO READERS

As a note to the readers, the story part about the track race a couple of years after graduating, playing football, and the football team singing "The Lord's Prayer" are true and made a lifetime impression on my heart and mind. It's as fresh in my memory today as if I was experiencing it all over again…yep, still gives me moose mump ories. The rest of the story has never happened outside of my own heart's desires and imagination as to how I wished my life with my kids and grandkids would have been, and pray this, coming from the Holy Spirit, is a prophetic message. God knows my heart and how we have settled this issue and that this prodigal son has been on this journey way too long and is over-ready to return home.

D E C E M B E R 6TH 2 0 0 7 …the date the play was finished, and this book began.

THANK YOU, JESUS!!!!

5 things for which I am thankful today!

1. My Lord and Savior Jesus Christ
2. My Faith and Family
3. The Creativity that the Holy Spirit has loaned me
4. My Three Children
5. My Grandchildren…God Bless them all

To my most recently born

GRANDCHILDREN

I thank God for the opportunity I get to tell you directly how special and loved you are by your G'pa Randy.

Matthew 6:9-13

This, then, is how you should pray:

Our Father who art in Heaven, hallowed be thy name, thy kingdom come, thy will be done on Earth as it is in Heaven. Give us this day our daily bread. Forgive us our debts, as we also have forgiven our debtors. And lead us not into temptation, but deliver us from evil. For if you forgive men when they sin against you, your heavenly Father will also forgive you. But if you do not forgive men their sins, your Father will not forgive your sins. For Thine is the Kingdom and the Power and the Glory forever... Amen!

Nowhere in the Bible did I ever see or hear of JESUS teaching or preaching and then saying... "If anyone has any needs, my Apostles and disciples will be down here on the left side of this hill to hear your complaints...I mean needs." JESUS always ministered to the people whom HE taught. That's why He, at times, needed to go away by Himself and pray so He could get renewed by His father, for how else would He know what His Father in Heaven desired. I pray it is our desire as well; I believe Jesus said,

"I only do that which I see my Father doing."
Amen!

The Lord's Prayer

Randall Lechner

PUBLISHED by PARABLES

Earthly Stories with a Heavenly Meaning